The Alpha Mechanic

A Protective Alpha Fated Mates
Steamy Omegaverse Romance

Ash Jade

D ear Reader,

Welcome to Sanctuary, a hidden mountain town whispered about in the wider omegaverse, a place where worn-down omegas come to heal and alphas learn that strength is measured in gentleness, not dominance. If you've made it this far, maybe part of you is curious... or hopeful... or simply ready to step into a world where instinct doesn't have to hurt, and where every story bends toward safety, connection, and a well-earned happily-ever-after.

Here, the omegaverse works a little differently.

Alphas, betas, and omegas still move through life guided by pheromones, instincts, and bonds, but Sanctuary is a refuge, one carved out of grief, rebuilt with stubborn hope, and held together by a pack that refuses to let anyone fall through the cracks. Heats and ruts still come like wild weather, but they're met with care, consent, and hands that steady instead of seize. And sometimes, the mountain air carries something more ancient still: the pull of fated mates, that quiet click inside your chest when you realize home might be a person as much as a place.

Each novella in this series is a fast, high-heat, heart-forward escape. A story about a protective alpha, a brave omega, and the slow re-teaching of trust. You can read them in order or wander in wherever you like. Every couple stands alone, yet each book threads another stitch into the found-family tapestry of Sanctuary.

Before you step inside, a few gentle warnings:

These stories contain explicit sexual content, primal dynamics, instinct-driven tension, and adult themes. They are not dark romance, but they *do* explore trauma recovery, vulnerability, and the process of learning to choose yourself again. Please honor your comfort level and step away if something doesn't sit right with you.

Additional content considerations: violence, injury, death, mentions of sexual violence (not depicted but discussed), and themes of healing from past harm.

If Sanctuary sounds like somewhere you might want to linger—if you're ready for protective alphas, fierce omegas, small-town gossip, soft pack dinners, and bonds that bloom where hurt once lived—then settle in.

The mountains are waiting.
— Ash Jade

Contents

1

— · —

The engine makes a sound no car should ever make—a metal-on-metal shriek that sends my hands clenching white-knuckled on the steering wheel. I wince, muttering curses under my breath as I ease off the gas. The mountains loom around me like silent judges, all gorgeous pines and clear skies that couldn't give less of a damn about my predicament. Then comes the smoke—thick, oily plumes erupting from under the hood. Just perfect.

"Not now, Betsy," I plead, patting the dashboard like it might respond to affection. "We're almost somewhere, I think."

The temperature gauge creeps steadily into the red. My faithful rustbucket chooses this moment—miles from anywhere I've ever been—to finally surrender to entropy. I've nursed this car through twelve states and more "check engine" lights than I can count, but this feels different. Terminal.

A green road sign appears around the curve: "Sanctuary - 1 mile."

"You hear that, girl? One more mile. You can do one more mile."

I shift into neutral, letting momentum and the downward slope carry us forward while the engine makes dying animal noises. The smoke thickens, and the stench of burning oil fills the car. I crack the window, gulping mountain air that tastes like pine and freedom—the exact things I'm chasing.

Or running toward. Or away from. Depends on the day.

Sanctuary unfolds ahead—a postcard-perfect small town nestled in the valley. Main Street stretches before me, lined with brick buildings, painted storefronts, and precisely zero chain establishments. The kind of place where everybody knows everybody's name, story, and probably their last three sexual partners. People like me never stay in towns like this.

I spot it just as Betsy gives a final, dramatic shudder—a weathered sign reading "Colt's Auto Repair" hanging above an old-fashioned garage. The universe's timing is either perfect or perfectly cruel.

"Hold on," I murmur, coasting on fumes and prayers.

I manage to steer into the parking lot before the engine dies completely. Betsy rolls to a stop, shuddering one final time before silence falls. Dead center of the lot. At least I didn't block anyone in.

I rest my forehead against the steering wheel and breathe. In through the nose, out through the mouth. My omega senses prickle with the vague scent markers of unfamiliar territory—predominantly alpha, which makes my skin tighten instinctively.

This wasn't the plan. My finger traces the folded map on the passenger seat—my route marked in bright green highlighter, with Sanctuary nowhere on it. Just another dot to pass through on my way to the coast and my next "adventure."

That's what I call them. Adventures. Sounds better than "desperate attempts to find somewhere I belong" or "places I stay until I inevitably fuck it up." Eight years of drifting, and I've gotten good at wearing my transience like a badge of honor instead of a wound.

I check my wallet—sixty-three dollars and a collection of loyalty cards to coffee shops I'll never visit again. My phone shows exactly two bars of service, which feels symbolic somehow.

"Okay, Sunny," I tell myself, using my cheerful voice—the one I've perfected for tight spots. "Just a quick fix, in and out. Your most charming self. You got this."

I fluff my unruly blonde curls in the rearview mirror and pinch color into my cheeks. The woman staring back has mastered the art of looking like she has her shit together when she absolutely does not. Twenty-seven years old with nothing to show for it but a dying car and a duffel bag of essentials in the back seat.

The suppressants should be masking most of my omega scent, but they're generic—the cheap kind that dull rather than eliminate. Any alpha with half-decent senses will clock me immediately. I dig through my purse for my emergency spray, giving myself a quick mist. Chemical pine. Delicious.

Outside, the garage is quiet. A couple of cars in various states of repair sit in the bays, but I don't see any mechanics. The place smells like motor oil, metal, and alpha—strong, territorial alpha. My omega hindbrain does an annoying little flutter that I ruthlessly squash.

I straighten my spine, paste on my best "I'm-not-actually-in-crisis" smile, and push open the car door. The heat hits me immediately—late summer in the mountains, surprisingly intense. Sweat prickles along my hairline as I slide out, my worn sneakers crunching on gravel.

"Hello?" I call out, my voice carrying across the lot. "Anybody home? I've got a bit of a situation here!"

I drum my fingers against my thigh, rehearsing my spiel. Car trouble, passing through, need it fixed yesterday, can't afford much but will work something out. The usual.

The garage door is open, dark and cool inside compared to the bright afternoon sun. I take a step toward it, preparing to unleash the full force of my charm offensive on whoever emerges.

"Just keep smiling," I whisper to myself. "One more fix, one more town, one more chance to hit the road."

Like always. Just one more adventure.

2

— • —

I shift my weight from foot to foot, squinting into the dimness of the garage. Metal clanks against concrete somewhere in the shadows. My omega instincts do an uncomfortable little twist, like a fish hook catching on tender flesh. I clear my throat, louder this time. "Hello? Stranded traveler in desperate need of vehicular resurrection over here!"

A grunt echoes from beneath a massive pickup truck. A pair of worn work boots stick out, attached to denim-clad legs. The boots slide forward as their owner pushes out from under the vehicle on a creeper.

Holy hell.

The alpha that emerges is a visual punch to my solar plexus. Six-foot-something of broad shoulders and barely contained strength. Dark hair cropped short, stubble darkening a jaw that could cut glass. His white t-shirt might've been clean this morning, but now it's smudged with grease that somehow makes him look more rugged rather than dirty. His scent hits me like a physical force—pine, metal, and something primal that makes my hindbrain sit up and beg.

He stands, wiping his hands on a rag, eyes narrowing as they land on me. They're a surprising color—amber, almost gold in the slanted light from the garage windows. The mechanic's expression shifts from mild annoyance to something sharper as he scents the air.

Shit. My suppressants are good, but not good enough to mask completely. Not for an alpha like this.

"Can I help you?" His voice is deep, rougher than gravel, and about as warm.

My mouth decides this is the perfect moment to divorce itself from my brain. "My car died! Well, not died-died, more like went into a coma after making noises a vehicle should never make, and then there was smoke—lots of smoke, which I'm pretty sure is universally bad news in the car world—and I was just passing through on my way to nowhere in particular because that's sort of my thing, you know, the whole footloose and fancy-free lifestyle, although right now it's feeling less free and more foot-stuck—"

I snap my mouth shut. His eyebrows have climbed steadily higher during my verbal avalanche.

"Your car." He points to poor Betsy, still steaming slightly in the parking lot.

"Yes. That's the one. My trusty steed. Though perhaps 'trusty' is generous at this point."

He walks past me, his arm brushing mine. The contact sends an electric jolt up my spine that I absolutely refuse to acknowledge. I trail after him like a lost puppy, which is embarrassing but unavoidable.

"I'm Sunny, by the way," I offer, stretching out my hand. "Just passing through."

He glances at my hand, then back at my face. After an awkward moment, he takes it. His palm is callused, warm, and engulfs mine completely. "Colt."

Of course his name is Colt. What else would you name a man who looks like he could tame wild horses with a glance?

He drops my hand quickly, turning his attention to my car. I watch as he pops the hood, cursing under his breath at the billowing steam that greets him. His movements are efficient, confident—the kind of capability that's weirdly attractive.

Not that I'm noticing.

"What brings you to Sanctuary?" he asks, not looking at me.

"Just driving through. I'm headed to the coast. Or was. Obviously, Betsy had other plans."

"Betsy?"

"The car. I name things. It's a quirk. Or a character flaw, depending who you ask."

He makes a noncommittal sound, leaning further under the hood. I catch myself staring at the way his shoulder blades move beneath his shirt and force my eyes away.

"You always travel alone?" The question sounds casual, but there's something else beneath it. Concern? Judgment?

"Yep. Just me, myself, and my stunning lack of mechanical knowledge."

Another grunt. He steps back, wiping his hands again. "Radiator's shot. Hose burst. Engine's overheated."

I wince. "That sounds expensive."

"It is."

Blunt. Great.

"How long will it take to fix?" I ask, trying to keep the desperation from my voice.

Colt studies me for a moment, his gaze uncomfortably perceptive. "Parts store closes in an hour. Won't have what I need today."

My stomach drops. "So tomorrow?"

"If I can get the parts in the morning."

I feel my smile falter. One night in this town means a motel. A motel means money I don't have. "Is there, um, is there somewhere cheap I could stay tonight?"

Something flickers across his face—a microexpression I can't interpret. He rubs the back of his neck, leaving a smudge of grease. "Motel on the edge of town. The Pinewood. It's basic but clean."

"Perfect." I nod too enthusiastically. "That sounds... attainably priced."

He stares at me, unblinking. His nostrils flare slightly, and I know he's picking up more than I want him to—stress, worry, the faint edge of fear that I can never quite shake when I'm somewhere new with no backup plan.

"I'll write up an estimate." He turns abruptly, heading back into the garage.

I follow, hugging myself despite the warm air. The garage interior is organized chaos—tools hung with military precision, parts stacked in labeled bins, an ancient radio playing classic rock from a high shelf. It smells like him in here, his alpha scent marking the territory as clearly as any sign.

He sits at a cluttered desk, pulling out a form. I hover awkwardly, too wired to sit, too intimidated to wander.

"You got someone you can call?" he asks without looking up.

"For what?"

"For help." Now he does look at me, those amber eyes assessing. "Money. A place to stay."

I laugh, the sound brittle even to my own ears. "No. Just me."

Something passes between us—a moment of recognition, perhaps. Lone wolves identifying each other in the wild.

"I'll have your car ready by tomorrow afternoon," he says finally, pushing the estimate toward me.

I look at the number and struggle not to visibly flinch. More than I have, but not as bad as I feared.

"Thanks," I manage, my cheerful mask slipping back into place. "I appreciate it."

He nods once, standing. We're close—too close in the confined space behind the desk. His scent wraps around me, making my omega instincts purr despite my brain's firm objections.

"Town's small," he says gruffly. "But safe. Diner down the street has good food."

Is he... being nice? Hard to tell through the grumpy alpha exterior.

"Right. Food. That's a thing people need." I step back, needing distance from his overwhelming presence. "I'll just... grab my bag and head to the motel. Left or right for the diner?"

"Left. Two blocks."

"Got it. Thanks, Colt."

As I turn to go, his voice stops me. "Sunny."

Just my name, but something in the way he says it makes my skin prickle with awareness.

"Yeah?"

"Be careful. Small towns notice strangers."

I can't tell if it's a warning or a threat. Either way, it follows me back to my car, settling like a weight between my shoulder blades.

3

—·—

I return to the garage with my tail between my legs, pride chewed up and spit out. The Pinewood Motel's neon vacancy sign mocked me with its $75-a-night rate—highway robbery for a place that probably hasn't seen new sheets since before I was born. The diner's coffee sits sour in my stomach, my last three dollars spent on a meal I barely tasted. Above me, the sky has transformed from postcard-perfect blue to something bruised and threatening. The air crackles with the promise of a storm—because clearly, my day hasn't gone sideways enough already.

Colt looks up from an engine part he's cleaning when I slip back inside. Surprise flickers across his face before the scowl returns.

"Thought you'd be at the motel by now," he says.

I force a laugh. "Change of plans. Turns out the Pinewood's rates are a bit rich for my blood." My attempt at casual falls flat. "Any chance you've worked a miracle on my car in the last hour?"

His hands still on the greasy component. "Called the parts store. They don't have what we need. Coming in from the next town over. Tomorrow morning, earliest."

"Oh." The single syllable drops like a stone.

"You got a plan B?" His voice is neutral, but his eyes are too observant, seeing too much.

I shrug with a nonchalance I don't feel. "Always. I'm considering my options."

"Which are?"

"Extensive and none of your business." I flash him a smile that doesn't reach my eyes.

He sets down the part and wipes his hands. Outside, thunder rumbles—closer than I expected. The garage lights flicker once, twice.

"Storm's coming in fast," Colt says, moving to the bay door. "Bad one, by the sound of it."

Great. Just what I need—to be homeless and drenched. I dig through my purse, taking inventory of my meager resources. Sixty dollars won't cover the motel, but maybe there's a cheaper place I haven't found. Or a shelter? Do towns this small even have shelters?

The first fat drops of rain hit the concrete outside with audible splats. Within seconds, it transforms into a downpour, sheets of water obscuring the world beyond the garage. Lightning flashes, illuminating Colt's profile as he watches the deluge. The thunder that follows is immediate and deafening.

"Jesus," I mutter, jumping despite myself.

"Direct hit," Colt says. "Power grid's shit here. We'll lose—"

The lights go out mid-sentence.

"—electricity," he finishes in the sudden darkness.

My eyes adjust slowly to the dim emergency lights casting everything in an eerie blue glow. Rain hammers against the metal roof, creating a cacophony that would be soothing if I wasn't busy having an internal panic attack about my situation.

Colt moves with surprising confidence through the dark garage, retrieving a flashlight from a drawer. The beam cuts through the gloom, landing briefly on my face before sweeping away.

"You can stay here," he says gruffly.

"What?"

"Tonight. You can stay here." He sounds like the words are being physically extracted from him. "Office has a couch. Not safe to be out in this."

My pride wars with practicality. Pride loses. "I couldn't impose—"

"Not an imposition. Common sense." He runs a hand through his short hair, a gesture that reads as discomfort. "I live upstairs. You take the office. Got a generator for essential power, but heat's electric. Might get cold."

I blink at him, trying to process this unexpected kindness from a man who's been radiating "go away" vibes since I arrived.

"Why would you do that?" The question slips out before I can stop it.

He looks at me, really looks at me, his amber eyes reflecting the emergency lights. "Because it's the right thing to do."

Simple. Straightforward. As if helping a stranded omega is the most natural thing in the world.

"Thank you," I say quietly, meaning it. "I'll be gone first thing in the morning."

He nods once, then gestures for me to follow him to the back of the garage. The office is small but neat—a desk with an ancient computer, filing cabinets, and a worn leather couch that's seen better days but looks clean enough.

"Bathroom's through there," he points to a door. "Got running water, even without power. Cold, though."

"I've had worse."

His eyebrow quirks, but he doesn't ask.

The storm rages outside, wind howling around the building's corners. Another crack of thunder makes me flinch. Colt notices—of course he does—but doesn't comment.

"I'll get you some blankets," he says, disappearing up a narrow staircase I hadn't noticed before.

Alone, I sink onto the couch, the leather cool against my jeans. The reality of my situation crashes over me—stranded in a strange town with a car I can't afford to fix, dependent on the charity of an alpha I met hours ago. My carefully constructed façade of carefree drifter crumbles a bit around the edges.

Colt returns with an armload of blankets and a pillow. They're worn but clean, and they smell like him—pine and motor oil and alpha. My omega hindbrain finds this absurdly comforting, which irritates my rational brain to no end.

"These should keep you warm enough," he says, dumping them on the couch beside me. "Generator will run the fridge and emergency lights, but that's about it."

"Better than camping," I offer with a weak smile.

"Done that often?"

"More times than I'd like to admit."

He nods like this makes perfect sense, then awkwardly hovers in the doorway. In the confined space of the office, his alpha presence seems magnified, filling every corner. I'm hyperaware of him—his height, his scent, the way his t-shirt stretches across his shoulders.

"There's food upstairs if you get hungry," he says finally. "Nothing fancy."

"I'm fine. Had dinner at the diner." The lie slips out as easily as breathing, and I'm not sure which of us I'm trying to convince—Colt, or myself. My stomach growls at the memory of watery coffee and the one free packet of crackers I'd managed to coax out of the bored server, but I ignore it. Food is a luxury I'll deal with tomorrow.

Colt regards me for a beat, alpha intuition clearly sensing the gap where honesty should be, but he lets it go with a grunt. Maybe he recognizes the pride in my tone, or maybe he's just as allergic to emotional displays as I am. He turns, boots thudding up the metal staircase at the back of the garage, and disappears into the gloom above.

The building settles around me, the storm outside battering the tin roof with relentless fury. Thunder rattles the windows in their frames and I flinch at every boom, cursing my jumpy nerves. I wrap myself tighter in the moth-soft blankets Colt left, trying not to inhale too greedily. The scent—him, and the faint trace of ozone from the storm—hits something deep in my animal wiring. I want to hate that, but the comfort is too raw and real to push away.

The office is silent except for the storm and the hum of the generator somewhere outside. I flip through my phone, hoping for distraction, but the battery is low and the WiFi predictably dead. Instead, I focus on the room: the battered desk, the wall calendar stuck forever on some distant year, the faded wanted poster pinned up as a joke. Colt's world, frozen in time, and now I'm an intruder in it.

I make a show of settling in—fluffing the pillow, arranging the blankets, even straightening the stack of invoices on the desk out of pure habit—but the adrenaline in my veins refuses to subside. I end up pacing the length of the office, then peeking into the bathroom, half-expecting to find it in horror-movie condition. It's surprisingly clean, if spartan. A cracked mirror, a sliver of soap, and a folded towel. I splash water on my face, the cold a bracing shock, and stare at my own reflection.

The woman staring back at me is thinner than she should be, smudges under her eyes and hair wild from the humidity. I force a smile—the mask I wear for the world—and it looks almost convincing in the half-light.

"You'll survive," I whisper to myself. "You always do."

Back in the office, I try to sleep. The couch groans beneath me, springs protesting every movement. I curl into a ball, listening to the storm and the distant creaks of the building settling under the wind's assault. Somewhere above, I hear the muffled sounds of Colt moving around—footsteps, a door closing, the low rumble of his voice on the phone. I wonder who he's talking to, what his story is. Why he offered to help me when he could have just locked the door and left me to the elements.

4

Sleep eludes me, skittering away like a spooked animal every time I close my eyes. The couch isn't uncomfortable, but my brain won't shut off. After an hour of staring at shadows dancing on the ceiling, I give up. The storm has settled into a steady rain, less dramatic but persistent. I wrap one of Colt's blankets around my shoulders like a cape and venture out of the office. The emergency lights cast blue-tinged shadows across the garage, transforming familiar shapes into something almost magical. I can't remember the last time I was alone in such a large, quiet space.

I trail my fingers along a workbench, examining tools I couldn't name if my life depended on it. Some are recognizable—wrenches, screwdrivers, hammers. Others look like medieval torture devices. I pick up something that resembles a metal claw, turning it over in my hands.

"That's a brake spring tool."

I startle, nearly dropping it. Colt stands at the foot of the stairs, wearing sweatpants and a faded t-shirt that's seen better days. His hair is mussed, like he's been running his hands through it. In the dim light, he looks softer somehow. Less intimidating.

"Sorry," I say, putting the tool back exactly where I found it. "Couldn't sleep."

"Me neither." He moves closer, picking up the tool. "This removes and installs the springs on drum brakes. Keeps your fingers intact."

"Handy. I'm rather attached to my fingers." I wiggle them for emphasis.

The ghost of a smile touches his lips. "You always wander around strange places in the middle of the night?"

"Only the interesting ones." I pull the blanket tighter around my shoulders. "What's that thing?" I point to a contraption hanging on the wall.

"Engine hoist. Pulls motors so I can work on them."

"And that?" I indicate another mysterious object.

"Timing light. Shows if the engine timing is correct."

I move around the garage, pointing at tools, parts, and half-finished projects. To my surprise, Colt answers each question patiently, sometimes demonstrating how something works. His voice loses its gruff edge when he talks about engines, becoming almost animated.

"You really love this stuff," I observe.

He shrugs, but I can tell it's true. "Been fixing things since I was a kid. Makes sense to me."

"Must be nice," I say without thinking. "Having something that makes sense."

He studies me, eyes curious in the blue light. "What makes sense to you?"

The question catches me off guard. "Movement, I guess. Not staying still long enough for things to get complicated."

"That makes sense to you? Always running?"

"I prefer to call it 'perpetual adventure.'"

"Same thing, different name."

I should be offended, but he's not wrong. "At least my name sounds more fun."

That almost-smile again. "Hungry? Got some vending machine stuff upstairs."

My stomach answers with an embarrassing growl. "Apparently, yes."

I follow him back up the narrow stairs to his apartment. It's small but surprisingly comfortable—an open living area with a kitchenette, a door that presumably leads to a bedroom, and a window seat overlooking the main street. The decor is minimal but not sterile. A bookshelf filled with actual books. A comfortable-looking couch. Signs of a life being lived, not just a place to crash.

Colt rummages in a cabinet, producing an array of vending machine snacks and two beers. "Gourmet dining at its finest."

"I'm not picky." I settle at his small kitchen table.

He joins me, pushing a bag of chips and a candy bar in my direction. "Sorry it's not more substantial."

"Are you kidding? This is the food of my people." I tear open the chips. "Road trip cuisine at its finest."

We eat in companionable silence for a few minutes. The rain taps gently against the windows, creating a cozy backdrop.

"So," he says finally. "Where were you headed before your car died?"

I shrug. "Wherever the road took me. I had a vague plan to hit the coast, find a beach town with seasonal work."

"You do that a lot? Just... drift?"

"It's my specialty. Eight years and counting." I try to make it sound like an accomplishment rather than a confession.

"What about before that?"

I pick at the label on my beer bottle. "Foster care. Aged out at eighteen, been on my own since."

His eyes soften with understanding, not pity. It's the only reason I don't immediately change the subject.

"Never wanted to settle somewhere?" he asks.

"Never found a place worth staying for." I take a swig of beer. "What about you? Always been in Sanctuary?"

He shakes his head. "Military first. Army. Four years."

That explains the precise way he organizes his tools, the economy of his movements.

"Came back here after?"

"Inherited the garage from my uncle. He took me in after my parents died when I was fifteen. Taught me everything I know."

I hear what he doesn't say—that this place is more than a business. It's a legacy, a connection to someone who mattered.

"You're good at it," I say. "Fixing things."

"Some things are easier to fix than others."

Our eyes meet across the table. A recognition of sorts.

"What's the strangest place you've been?" he asks, surprising me with his continued interest.

I grin. "Okay, strangest place I ever stayed? There was this commune in New Mexico—three weeks of my life I'll never get back. I learned how to make goat cheese and almost accidentally joined a cult."

Colt actually laughs, the sound deep and rusty, like it hasn't seen daylight in years. "A cult?"

I nod, trying not to laugh myself. "Yeah. They called it a 'wellness retreat,' but honestly? If I'd stayed any longer I'd probably be wearing linen and selling essential oils out of an RV."

His mouth quirks. "Did you at least keep the goat cheese recipe?"

"I did. But it tastes better with freedom."

I find myself telling him about the series of odd jobs I've held—waitress, fruit picker, dog walker, temporary office assistant, house sitter. The constant motion, never staying anywhere long enough to put down roots. I don't tell him about the fear that drives me, the sense that if I stay too long, I'll either be rejected or hurt. Some truths are too raw for midnight confessions.

In return, he tells me about Sanctuary—the quirky townspeople, the seasonal tourists, the rhythm of life in a place where everyone knows everyone else.

"Sounds suffocating," I say.

"Can be," he admits. "But there's something to knowing where you belong."

"Is that what it feels like? Belonging?"

He considers this, his amber eyes thoughtful. "Most days. It's not perfect, but it's home."

Home. Such a simple word, yet it lodges in my chest like a splinter. I've never had a home, not really. Just places I've stayed.

"The thing about small towns," Colt says, popping the last piece of chocolate in his mouth, "is that they can surprise you. Sanctuary's got its share of gossips and busybodies, but when someone needs help? Everyone shows up."

I think about his offer to let me stay tonight, made gruffly but without hesitation. "Like you did for me."

He looks almost embarrassed. "Anyone would've done the same."

"No," I say with the certainty of someone who's been left stranded before. "They wouldn't."

Our eyes meet again, and this time the connection feels deeper, more meaningful. I see something in his gaze—a caring heart carefully hidden behind walls of self-protection. It mirrors something in me, and the recognition is both comforting and terrifying.

The moment stretches between us, taut with possibility. Then he clears his throat, breaking the spell.

"Should try to get some sleep," he says, gathering the empty wrappers. "Parts store opens at eight."

I nod, suddenly aware of how comfortable I've become in his presence. How easily I've shared things I rarely tell anyone. How the knot of tension I've carried between my shoulders for miles has loosened.

"Thanks," I say as I stand. "For the five-star accommodations and gourmet dining experience."

His lips quirk. "Anytime."

It's just a word, a polite nothing, but for a heartbeat, I let myself imagine what it would be like to take him up on it. To have an "anytime" with someone.

Dangerous thinking for a drifter.

I wrap the blanket tighter around me and head back downstairs, oddly reluctant to leave his space—the first place in a very long time that's felt, even fleetingly, like it could be safe.

5

— · —

Morning arrives with grudging sunlight and the aftermath of the storm—branches scattered across the parking lot, puddles reflecting the clearing sky. I've been awake for hours, pretending to sleep on Colt's office couch, my mind racing with thoughts I have no business entertaining. The night's conversation left me feeling exposed, like I'd accidentally revealed more of myself than intended. Dangerous territory for someone who survives by keeping people at arm's length. I hear Colt moving around upstairs and steel myself for the day ahead—get the car fixed, get back on the road, get away from this alpha who somehow slipped past my usual defenses.

By the time I fold the blankets and splash cold water on my face in the tiny bathroom, Colt has already come downstairs. He's back in work clothes—jeans and a different grease-stained t-shirt—and he's made coffee. The rich scent fills the garage, momentarily overpowering the oil and metal smells.

"Morning," he says, voice rougher than usual. "Sleep okay?"

"Like a baby," I lie, accepting the mug he offers. "Storm kept you up too?"

He grunts noncommittally, not meeting my eyes. Something's different about him this morning—a tension in his shoulders, a tightness around his mouth. I chalk it up to the awkwardness of having a stranger invade his space.

"Parts store opens in thirty," he says, checking his watch. "Got some eggs upstairs if you're hungry."

"Coffee's fine for now." I take a sip, surprised by how good it is. "Wow. This doesn't taste like it came from a gas station."

That hint of a smile. "Local roaster. One of the few perks of small-town living."

We eat breakfast in his apartment—scrambled eggs and toast, because Colt insisted and my stomach betrayed me with another embarrassing growl. The conversation is stilted compared to last night's easy flow, both of us carefully navigating around the unexpected intimacy we'd shared.

"I'll clean up," I say when we finish, gathering the plates. "Least I can do."

He hesitates like he wants to argue, then nods, checking his phone. "I'll call the parts store, see if our order came in."

I stand at his tiny sink, washing dishes, oddly domestic in a stranger's space. Outside, Sanctuary is waking up—I can see the main street from the window, people moving along the sidewalks, a normalcy I've always observed from the outside.

Colt ends his call and joins me at the sink, reaching past me for a dishtowel. "Part's in. I'll head over—"

His arm brushes mine, and the world stops.

Heat explodes where our skin touches, a jolt of electricity that races up my arm and spreads through my entire body. My breath catches. His scent—which I'd been carefully ignoring—suddenly intensifies, overwhelming my senses. Pine and metal and alpha, but with a new note—something primal and musky that makes my knees weak.

The plate slips from my fingers, clattering back into the sink.

Colt freezes, his body going rigid. I hear his sharp intake of breath, see his pupils dilate. His nostrils flare as he scents me—really scents me—and I realize with horror what's happening.

My suppressants are failing.

The cheap, generic pills I've been taking—stretching out to save money—have chosen this moment to stop working. My omega pheromones are broadcasting loud and clear, and judging by Colt's reaction, the message is coming through with terrifying clarity.

"Fuck," he mutters, stepping back so quickly he bumps into the counter behind him. "You're—"

"On suppressants," I say quickly, desperately. "They're working fine."

We both know I'm lying. The air between us is thick with pheromones—his and mine, calling to each other in a primal conversation our conscious minds are trying to ignore.

"Your rut," I say, the realization hitting me. "It's starting."

He runs a hand over his face, turning away from me. "Not supposed to. Not for weeks."

But it is. I can smell it—that distinctive alpha-in-rut scent that's always sent me running in the opposite direction. Except my body isn't telling me to run. It's telling me to get closer, to press myself against him, to bare my neck and—

No. Absolutely not.

I back away, putting the small kitchen table between us. "I should go."

"Go where?" His voice is strained, deeper than before. "Your car's still dead."

Reality crashes back. I'm stranded in a small town with no money, no transportation, and an alpha mechanic whose rut I've apparently triggered. Perfect.

"I'll figure something out. I always do." The bravado in my voice sounds hollow even to my own ears.

Colt grips the edge of the counter, knuckles white. I watch his chest rise and fall with deliberately measured breaths. He's fighting it—fighting his instincts. The realization both relieves and oddly disappoints me.

"It's the mate pull," he says finally, the words forced out like they're physically painful. "You feel it too."

I want to deny it, but what's the point? My body is betraying me with every heartbeat, responding to his presence in ways I've never experienced before. Heat pools low in my belly. My pulse races. My skin feels too tight, too sensitive.

"It doesn't mean anything," I say fiercely. "Biology, not destiny. Just pheromones and primitive instincts."

"Right." He nods too quickly. "Exactly."

"I've met alphas before whose ruts synced with me. It happens. Doesn't mean we're—" I can't even say the word.

"Of course not." He still won't look at me directly. "I'll get the part. Fix your car. You can be on your way."

"Good. Great. Perfect plan."

We stand in awkward silence, the small apartment suddenly feeling like a cage. I'm acutely aware of every movement he makes, every breath. I can hear his heartbeat—or maybe it's mine, pounding in my ears.

I think of other alphas I've encountered—the ones who took an omega's heat as permission, not a responsibility. The ones who believed their rut entitled them to whatever they wanted. The ones I've been running from my entire adult life.

Colt doesn't seem like that. But they never do, at first.

"I had an alpha professor once," I say, the words tumbling out, "who said omega pheromones triggered his rut. Used it as an excuse to corner me in his office. Told me I was asking for it just by existing."

Colt's head snaps up, his eyes blazing with something that looks like anger but not directed at me. "That's not—I would never—"

"I know." And strangely, I do know. Despite everything, despite all my hard-earned caution, I believe him. "But this still isn't happening."

He nods, visibly gathering his control. "I'll go get the part. Start working on your car."

"I'll stay down in the office."

"Good idea."

Neither of us moves. The air between us vibrates with unspoken possibilities, with needs neither of us is willing to acknowledge. My omega instincts whine for his touch, begging me to close the distance. I dig my nails into my palms, the pain grounding me.

"Sunny," he says, my name rough in his throat.

"Don't." I shake my head. "Just... don't."

He understands. With visible effort, he walks past me to the door, careful to keep space between us. I feel his heat as he passes, catch another wave of his scent. My body sways toward him involuntarily.

"Lock the door behind me," he says, hand on the doorknob. "I'll knock when I get back."

I nod, not trusting my voice.

When he's gone, I sink into a kitchen chair, my legs suddenly unable to support me. I press my hands to my burning cheeks, reality crashing over me in waves.

Mate pull. The thing every unbonded omega both dreads and secretly hopes for. The biological imperative that overrides reason, that draws compatible pairs together with irresistible force.

I've spent my life avoiding attachment, keeping people at arm's length, never staying long enough to form connections. And now my traitorous body has decided this gruff, reluctant alpha is the one I'm meant for?

Not happening. Not now, not ever.

I just need to get my car fixed and get out of Sanctuary before these feelings—these instincts—become impossible to ignore.

Before I do something truly stupid, like wonder what it would be like to stay.

6

The first cramp hits me like a sucker punch. I double over on the office couch, a gasp escaping before I can trap it behind my teeth. No. Not now. Not here. But my body doesn't care about convenient timing. Heat rushes through me in a merciless wave, turning my skin to live wires, my blood to magma. I press my face into the cushion, inhaling Colt's lingering scent—a mistake that sends another spasm of need coursing through me. The suppressants haven't just failed. They've catastrophically backfired, triggering a heat more intense than any I've experienced before.

I've been hiding in the office for hours, pretending to read outdated car magazines while Colt works on Betsy outside. The storm has returned, rain lashing against the windows in sheets. The power flickered back on around noon, but the garage remains eerily quiet except for the occasional clang of tools and muttered curse from the service bay.

Another cramp twists my insides. I curl into myself, biting my lip until I taste blood. This isn't the gradual onset I'm used to—the slow build of warmth and desire that gives me time to find somewhere safe, somewhere private. This is a tsunami, overwhelming and unstoppable.

My omega pheromones must be flooding the small space. Even I can smell them—sweet and ripe and desperate. How long before they reach Colt? Before his already-triggered rut responds to the unmistakable scent of an omega in heat?

I need to leave. Now. Before things get worse.

I force myself to stand, legs trembling. My skin feels too tight, too hot. Every fiber of my clothing scrapes like sandpaper. I grab my duffel bag, not sure where I'm going but certain I can't stay.

The office door opens.

Colt stands frozen in the doorway, a greasy rag in one hand, the other white-knuckled on the doorframe. His eyes widen, nostrils flaring as my scent hits him like a physical force. His pupils dilate instantly, black swallowing amber.

"Sunny." My name is a growl, barely human.

"Don't." I back away until I hit the desk. "Stay there."

He doesn't move, but his chest heaves with labored breaths. I can see him fighting his instincts—fighting the alpha urge to claim, to possess. His scent has changed, intensified, the rut pheromones triggering another wave of heat that makes me whimper despite my best efforts.

"You're in heat," he says unnecessarily, his voice deeper than I've ever heard it.

"Really? I hadn't noticed." Even now, I can't help the sarcasm. "I was just leaving."

"In this?" He gestures to the window, where rain lashes horizontally across the glass. "Where would you even go?"

"Anywhere." Another cramp doubles me over. "Just—away."

I see the moment his alpha instincts register my pain. Something primal and protective flashes across his face. He takes a half-step forward before catching himself.

"Let me help," he says, then immediately clarifies: "Not like that. Medicine. Water. Food. Whatever you need."

I've heard those words before. From an alpha ex who thought "helping" meant taking what he wanted. From a landlord who suggested I could "work off" my rent during my heat. From countless men who saw my biology as an invitation rather than a vulnerability.

"I don't need an alpha's help," I spit, anger temporarily overriding pain.

Colt flinches like I've slapped him. "I'm not—" He stops, takes a deep breath. "Okay. No help. But you can't leave in this storm. And I can't..." He runs a hand through his hair, agitated. "I can't be near you like this."

He turns abruptly, walking out and closing the door behind him. I hear his footsteps retreat, then the sound of the exterior door opening and closing.

Confused, I move to the window. Through the rain-streaked glass, I see Colt standing in the downpour, face tilted up, letting the cold water soak him. His fists clench and unclench at his sides. He's giving himself space—giving me space—despite the biological imperative screaming at him to do otherwise.

It's the most respect any alpha has ever shown me during heat.

I sink back to the couch as another wave hits. My body feels hollow, aching for something—someone. The emptiness is physical pain, my omega biology demanding satisfaction.

Minutes pass. Maybe hours. Time blurs as the heat takes hold. I drift in and out of awareness, conscious only of need and the struggle against it.

The office door opens again. Colt stands there, dripping wet but calmer. His eyes are still dark with rut, but his breathing is controlled. In his hands is a tray with water bottles, protein bars, and what looks like pain relievers.

"May I?" he asks, not entering without permission.

I nod weakly.

He sets the tray on the desk, careful to keep distance between us. "These should help with the symptoms. Not much, but something."

"Thank you." The words come out hoarse.

"I'll be upstairs." He backs toward the door. "Lock this behind me. I won't—I won't come down unless you call."

I stare at him, this alpha fighting his own biology to respect my boundaries. It's so unexpected I momentarily forget the fire consuming me from inside.

"Why?" I ask. "Why fight it? Most alphas wouldn't."

His jaw tightens. "I'm not most alphas."

Four simple words, yet they hold a weight, a promise. I believe him, and that terrifies me more than the heat itself.

He leaves, and I drag myself to the door to lock it as instructed. The simple act of moving sends fresh waves of need through me. I collapse back to the couch, curling around a pillow that smells like Colt.

Through the ceiling, I hear him pacing. The rhythmic sound of his footsteps is oddly comforting—he's still there, still fighting, still resisting the call of my pheromones.

Outside, thunder cracks again, the storm returning with renewed fury. It matches the tempest inside me—wild, uncontrollable, elemental. Lightning flashes, briefly illuminating the office in stark white. In that moment of clarity, I admit what I've been denying since our hands touched this morning.

The mate pull is real. My body recognizes what my mind refuses to accept—that this gruff, reluctant alpha is my biological match. That my omega instincts are screaming for him specifically, not just any alpha.

But biology isn't destiny. I've survived worse than this. I'll ride out the heat alone, as I always have. And when it's over, I'll leave Sanctuary behind like every other place.

Another cramp, worse than before. I bite into the pillow to muffle my cry. Through the pain comes a treacherous thought: What if I didn't have to suffer alone? What if, just this once, I trusted an alpha during my most vulnerable time?

I shake my head violently. That way lies danger. Attachment. Everything I've spent years avoiding.

Above me, Colt's pacing grows more agitated. I hear something crash, followed by a low, frustrated growl that vibrates through the floorboards and straight to my core. My body responds instantly, slick warmth between my thighs, a whimper escaping my lips.

He must hear it—his alpha senses heightened by rut—because the pacing stops. For several heartbeats, the only sounds are the storm and our matched breathing, somehow audible to each other despite the distance.

"Sunny?" His voice reaches me through the floor, strained and rough.

"I'm okay," I call back, the lie transparent even to my own ears.

Another growl, this one deeper. Possessive. Protective. My omega instincts respond with a surge of need so intense it brings tears to my eyes.

The storm rages outside, but the real tempest is within these walls—two people fighting their most primal instincts, separated by a single floor and a lifetime of caution. The tension builds with each passing minute, each labored breath, each wave of pheromones.

I press my face into the pillow, breathing in Colt's scent, allowing myself just this small indulgence. My resolve wavers like a candle flame in the wind. For the first time since my car broke down, I wonder if Sanctuary might have brought me exactly where I need to be.

That thought is more frightening than any heat.

7

— · —

Hour three, and my heat has become a living thing—a beast clawing me from the inside out. I've soaked through my clothes with sweat, the couch cushions damp beneath me. Every nerve ending screams for relief. The pain medication Colt left did nothing; the water bottles are empty, crushed in my desperate grip. I've tried everything—cold compresses, pressure against my abdomen, even the embarrassing friction of grinding against the couch cushions. Nothing helps. This heat is different—stronger, more focused. My body knows what it wants. Who it wants. And my mind is losing the battle to deny it.

Lightning cracks outside, thunder following almost instantly. The storm mirrors the chaos inside me—wild, elemental, beyond control. Another cramp tears through me, and this time I can't hold back the sob that follows.

Above me, I hear Colt's footsteps stop. He's been pacing relentlessly, his own battle evidently as difficult as mine. In the sudden silence, I can almost feel him listening, attuned to my every sound.

"Sunny?" His voice carries through the floor, strained almost beyond recognition.

I don't answer. Can't answer. The pain recedes momentarily, leaving in its wake a moment of startling clarity. Like the eye of the storm, a brief respite that allows one coherent thought to form.

This isn't going away. Not without help. His help.

Eight years of running. Eight years of keeping people at arm's length. Eight years of handling my heats alone, suffering through them with gritted teeth and the conviction that needing no one was strength. But maybe—just maybe—there's strength in choosing to trust, too.

I've never wanted anyone the way I want Colt right now. Not just as an alpha, not just as biological relief, but as himself—the man who stood in the rain rather than take advantage, who brought me supplies and respected my boundaries, who fights his instincts even now.

My body has already made its choice. Perhaps it's time my mind caught up.

I force myself to stand on trembling legs. The simple cotton dress I changed into clings to my sweat-soaked skin. My hair is a wild tangle around my face. I must look feral, desperate.

I am both of those things, but something else too—resolved.

The stairs are a mountain to climb. Each step sends fresh waves of need coursing through me. I grip the railing so hard my knuckles go white. At the top, I pause, gathering what little composure remains.

I don't knock. Just turn the handle and step inside.

Colt whirls toward me, eyes wild, chest heaving. The apartment is in disarray—a chair overturned, books swept from shelves, signs of his struggle for control. He's stripped to just his jeans, his chest bare and gleaming with sweat. The sight of him hits me like a physical blow.

"You shouldn't be here," he growls, backing away until he hits the wall. "I can't—"

"I want you to." My voice is steadier than I expected. "I'm choosing this. Choosing you."

He shakes his head, even as his body strains toward me. "The heat—you're not thinking clearly—"

"I've never been clearer." I take a step closer. "I know what I'm asking. I know what it means."

"Sunny." My name is a prayer and a curse on his lips. "If I touch you now, I won't be able to stop."

"I don't want you to stop."

The last thread of his control snaps visibly. He crosses the room in two strides, gathering me against him with a force that should frighten me but instead feels like coming home. His mouth crashes onto mine, hungry and demanding. I open for him immediately, my body singing with relief at finally, finally getting what it craves.

His hands are everywhere—tangling in my hair, skimming down my back, cupping my ass to pull me tighter against him. I moan into his mouth as his hardness presses against my stomach, proof of his desire, his need matching mine.

"Too many clothes," he mutters against my lips, bunching the fabric of my dress in his fists.

The sound of tearing cloth should upset me, but all I feel is relief as cool air hits my fevered skin. My dress falls away in tatters, leaving me in just my underwear—already soaked through with slick. Colt growls at the sight, a primal sound that sends a fresh wave of heat through me.

"Bedroom," I gasp as his mouth finds my neck, teeth grazing the sensitive spot where my bond mark would go.

He growls. Before I can process his meaning, he lifts me effortlessly, carrying me back down the stairs.

The garage is dark except for the emergency lights, blue-tinged shadows dancing as lightning flashes through the windows. Rain hammers against the metal roof, creating a primal soundtrack to our desperation. Colt sets me on his workbench, tools clattering to the floor as he sweeps them aside.

The metal is cold against my heated skin, a shocking contrast that pulls a gasp from my throat. Colt's hands bracket my thighs, pushing them apart to make space for his hips. His eyes never leave mine as he pops the button on his jeans.

"Last chance," he says, his voice wrecked. "Tell me to stop and I will."

Even now—even with his rut in full swing—he's giving me a choice. Something breaks open in my chest, a warmth that has nothing to do with heat and everything to do with trust.

"Don't stop," I whisper, reaching for him. "Please, Colt. I need you."

His jeans hit the floor. He tears my underwear away like tissue paper. Then he's there, the blunt head of his cock pressing against my entrance, already slick and ready for him.

"Mine," he growls as he pushes inside in one powerful thrust.

The stretch burns, perfect and overwhelming. I cry out, nails digging into his shoulders as he fills me completely. For one heart-stopping moment, he's still—both of us adjusting to the intensity of our connection. Then he begins to move, and coherent thought dissolves.

Each thrust drives me higher, closer to the edge I've been hovering near for hours. My heat responds to his rut, my body producing more slick, my inner walls clenching around him like we were made for this—for each other. The workbench creaks beneath us, tools rattling with each powerful drive of his hips.

"So perfect," he murmurs against my throat, one hand tangling in my hair to tilt my head back, exposing my neck. "So fucking perfect for me."

His teeth graze my pulse point—not biting, not yet, but the promise of it sends electric shivers down my spine. I wrap my legs around his waist, pulling him deeper, urging him on with breathless pleas.

Outside, thunder crashes directly overhead. The storm has found us, circling this garage where two strangers surrender to something ancient and undeniable. Lightning illuminates Colt's face above me—his eyes nearly black with desire, jaw clenched with restraint even now. He's holding back, I realize. Even lost in rut, he's careful with me.

"Don't," I gasp, arching against him. "Don't hold back. I won't break."

Something fierce and beautiful crosses his face. He hooks his arms under my knees, changing the angle, driving impossibly deeper. Each thrust hits a spot inside me that sends white-hot pleasure racing through my veins. I'm climbing, climbing, the peak just out of reach.

"That's it," he encourages, his rhythm faltering as his own release approaches. "Let go, Sunny. I've got you."

His thumb finds my clit, circling roughly, and I shatter. My orgasm tears through me with shocking intensity, wave after wave of pleasure so powerful I scream his name. My inner walls clamp down on him, triggering his own release. He growls, burying himself to the hilt as his cock pulses inside me.

Then I feel it—the swelling at the base of his shaft, his knot expanding, locking us together in the most primal way. The pressure against my sensitive tissues triggers another orgasm, smaller but no less intense. I cling to him, trembling, as he carefully maneuvers us into a more comfortable position with me sitting on his lap, still joined intimately.

"Fuck," he whispers against my hair, cradling me close as his knot ties us together. "Sunny..."

Just my name, but it contains a universe of meaning. I press my face against his chest, listening to his thundering heartbeat gradually slow. The storm continues outside, but inside, a different kind of peace settles over us.

I've never been knotted before. Never trusted an alpha enough to allow it. The sensation is strange but not unpleasant—a fullness, a connection beyond the physical. Colt's arms tighten around me, his cheek resting on top of my head. His scent has changed, mellowed slightly with satisfaction but still tinged with the musk of rut. It will return full force soon enough, as will my heat. But for now, we have this moment of clarity.

"Are you okay?" he asks, voice soft with concern. His hand strokes gently up and down my spine.

I nod against his chest, not ready to face him yet. The intensity of what just happened—what we just shared—overwhelms me. Not just the physical release, but the emotional connection that came with it. I didn't expect that. Didn't prepare for it.

"I didn't hurt you?" His worry is palpable.

I shake my head. "No. Just the opposite."

His knot will take time to go down. We're locked together, literally and perhaps in ways I'm not ready to examine. The implications terrify me—mate pull, biological compatibility, the possibility of something I've never allowed myself to want.

Outside, the storm begins to recede, thunder rumbling in the distance now. Inside, pressed against Colt's chest with his heartbeat steady beneath my ear, I face a truth I've been running from for years:

Some connections can't be outrun, no matter how fast or far you drive.

8

— · —

Colt's knot finally releases, our bodies separating with a rush of warmth that should be embarrassing but somehow isn't. My muscles ache pleasantly, my heat temporarily sated. I expect awkwardness—the sudden realization of what we've done, the inevitable regret that follows losing control. Instead, Colt gathers me against his chest with a gentleness that catches me off guard. His lips brush my forehead, my temple, the curve of my cheek—soft, reverent touches that have nothing to do with lust and everything to do with care.

"Can you stand?" he asks, voice gravelly but tender.

I nod, though I'm not entirely sure. My legs feel like jelly, my entire body buzzing with aftershocks of pleasure. He helps me down from the workbench, steadying me when I wobble.

"I've got you," he murmurs, and the simple phrase unlocks something in my chest.

I've never had this—the after. I've always handled my heats alone or slipped away from meaningless hookups before the sweat could dry. But Colt wraps an arm around my waist, supporting my weight as he leads me to the small bathroom off the garage.

"Wait here," he says, sitting me on the closed toilet lid. He disappears, returning moments later with a clean towel and a fresh t-shirt—his, by the size of it.

What happens next stuns me more than any orgasm. Colt wets a washcloth with warm water and kneels before me. With heartbreaking tenderness, he cleans between my thighs, his touch clinical but gentle. No alpha has ever cared for my body this way—as something precious rather than merely useful.

I should be mortified. Instead, I find myself blinking back unexpected tears.

"You okay?" he asks, instantly alert to my shift in mood. "Did I hurt you?"

"No," I manage, voice thick. "Just... not used to this part."

Understanding darkens his eyes. His hand cups my cheek, thumb brushing away moisture I didn't realize had escaped. "You should be. You deserve to be taken care of."

Simple words. Life-altering ones.

He helps me into his t-shirt, the soft cotton falling to mid-thigh. It smells like him, and my omega hindbrain purrs with satisfaction at being wrapped in my alpha's scent.

My alpha. The thought should terrify me. It does, but not in the way I expected.

"You need to hydrate," Colt says, practical again. "And eat something. Heat burns calories like crazy."

He leads me upstairs to his apartment, one arm constantly supporting me. The storm has passed again, leaving a gentle rain pattering against the windows.

Colt sits me at the kitchen table and brings me water, watching until I drain the glass. He refills it immediately, then rummages in his refrigerator.

"Not much here," he apologizes. "But I can make eggs and toast again. Protein's good for heat recovery."

"You seem to know a lot about it," I observe.

He shrugs, cracking eggs into a bowl. "Had an omega sister. Learned what helps."

"Had?" I ask before I can stop myself.

"She died. Car accident. Five years ago." His voice is flat, but I see the grief in the tight line of his shoulders.

"I'm sorry." Inadequate words for such a loss.

He nods once, acknowledging but not inviting further discussion. Another thing I appreciate about him—he doesn't demand emotional labor when I'm already drained.

We eat in comfortable silence. The food is simple but exactly what my body needs. I feel strength returning to my limbs, the fog of heat-madness temporarily lifting. I know it will return—heats typically last three days, sometimes longer—but for now, I have clarity.

"Your car," Colt says suddenly. "I got the part before... before everything. I can finish the repairs tomorrow."

Reality crashes back. My car. The road. My life of perpetual movement. It all seems strangely distant now, like a life that belongs to someone else.

"Thank you," I say, meaning it for more than just the car repair.

He studies my face, those amber eyes seeing too much. "What happens after?"

The question hanging between us. Will I stay or will I go?

"I don't know." For once, it's the absolute truth. "I haven't thought that far ahead."

"No need to decide now." He takes our empty plates to the sink. "Your heat will last another day or two. We can figure things out after."

We. Such a small word to hold so much potential.

A wave of exhaustion hits me suddenly, my body demanding rest before the next round of heat. Colt notices immediately—of course he does.

"You should sleep while you can," he says. "Heat's like that—intense peaks, then crashes."

"I know how heat works," I say, but there's no bite to it.

He smiles—a real one this time, not just the hint I've glimpsed before. It transforms his face, softening the hard lines, revealing the man beneath the gruff exterior. "Of course you do. Come on."

I expect him to lead me to his bedroom. Instead, he takes me back downstairs to the office.

"You'll be more comfortable here," he explains, arranging fresh blankets on the couch. "My bed reeks of alpha rut. Might trigger your heat again before you've rested."

His consideration floors me. Every alpha I've encountered during heat has been focused solely on their pleasure, their convenience. Colt puts my needs first in ways I didn't know were possible.

I sink onto the couch, suddenly too tired to stand. Colt tucks the blankets around me with surprising deftness.

"Will you stay?" I ask, the request slipping out before I can censor it.

He hesitates. "Are you sure? I don't want to crowd you."

"I'm sure." And I am. Despite everything, despite years of keeping my distance, I want him near.

He settles into the desk chair, close enough to reach out and touch but giving me space. His scent wraps around me, comforting rather than arousing now that my heat has temporarily receded.

"Get some sleep," he says softly. "I'll be here when you wake up."

Such a simple promise, yet it means everything. In my world of constant motion, of never staying long enough to form attachments, the idea of someone being there when I wake is both foreign and achingly desirable.

I watch him through heavy-lidded eyes as sleep pulls me under. He sits quietly, vigilant, protective. His presence doesn't feel threatening or constraining as I always feared an alpha's would. Instead, it feels like safety—a concept so unfamiliar I almost don't recognize it.

As I drift off, one thought follows me into dreams: beneath his gruff exterior, Colt might be the safest place I've ever found.

The realization should send me running. Instead, for the first time in years, I feel the urge to stay.

9

I wake to sunlight streaming through the office blinds, momentarily confused by unfamiliar surroundings. The couch creaks as I stretch, muscles pleasantly sore in ways that trigger an immediate flush of memories. Colt's hands. His mouth. The workbench. Heat rushes to my cheeks as fragments of last night flash through my mind with high-definition clarity. I'm alone in the office, but evidence of Colt's presence remains—a fresh water bottle on the desk, my clothes cleaned and folded neatly on a chair, his scent lingering on the blanket wrapped around me.

My heat has temporarily receded, giving me a window of lucidity before the next wave hits. I sit up, running fingers through my tangled hair, trying to gather my thoughts. What happens now? The script for one-night stands is clear—thank you, goodbye, never look back. But this wasn't just a hookup. It was heat and rut, alpha and omega, mate pull and primal connection.

And I'm still here, in his garage, wearing his shirt.

I grab my clothes, ducking into the small bathroom to change. My reflection startles me—cheeks flushed, eyes bright, lips slightly swollen. I look... different. Not just physically, but something deeper. Like something fundamental has shifted.

"Get it together, Sunny," I mutter to my reflection. "It was just biology."

The lie tastes bitter even as I think it.

I hear movement upstairs, the creak of floorboards announcing Colt's presence. Anxiety flutters in my stomach. What do you say to someone who's seen you at your most vulnerable, most primal? Someone whose knot you took less than twelve hours after meeting them?

My default setting kicks in—deflect with humor, keep it light, don't let them see you care.

I climb the stairs, each step a battle between turning back and moving forward. The door at the top is ajar. I knock lightly before pushing it open.

"So," I say with forced brightness, "do you offer breakfast to all the omegas you knot on workbenches, or am I special?"

Colt stands at the small stove, spatula in hand, wearing jeans and a fresh t-shirt. He turns at my voice, and the look on his face stops my nervous babbling cold. No disgust. No regret. No dismissal. Just warmth, concern, and something deeper, softer.

"Just you," he says simply.

"Oh." My clever retorts desert me. "That's... good."

He gestures to the table, already set with plates and cutlery. "Hungry?"

I nod, sitting down as he slides perfectly cooked eggs onto my plate, along with toast and what smells like real bacon. My stomach growls appreciatively.

"Your heat will cycle back soon," he says, joining me at the table. "Food helps maintain your strength between waves."

"You really do know a lot about this," I observe, digging into the eggs.

"Told you. Sister." His answers are still clipped, but not unkind. Just his way.

We eat in silence, but it's not uncomfortable. That's new for me—being able to share quiet space with someone without the compulsion to fill it with chatter. Colt doesn't demand conversation. He simply sits across from me, his presence solid and reassuring.

When we finish, he takes our plates to the sink. "I'm going to work on your car."

For some reason, this simple statement sends a pang through me. My car. My ticket out of here. Back to the road, to drifting, to nowhere in particular.

"Can I watch?" I ask impulsively.

He looks surprised but nods. "If you want."

I follow him downstairs, careful to avoid looking at the workbench where we... where it happened. The garage looks different in daylight—more ordinary, less the site of primal transformation. Colt moves to Betsy, popping the hood with practiced ease.

I perch on a nearby stool, drawing my knees up to my chest. There's something hypnotic about watching him work—the sure movements of his hands, the focused concentration on his face. He doesn't talk much, occasionally naming a part or explaining what he's doing, but mostly he works in silence.

I should be planning my departure. Calculating how far I can get on what's left in my wallet. Thinking about my next adventure. Instead, I find myself studying the way sunlight plays across Colt's shoulders, the tiny scar above his right eyebrow, the careful way he handles even the smallest components.

"Almost done," he says after an hour, not looking up from the engine. "Radiator's fixed. Just need to refill the coolant and test it."

"You make it look easy."

He shrugs. "Just practice. Anyone can learn."

"Not me. I once tried to change my own oil and ended up with a small environmental disaster in a Walmart parking lot."

That earns me a smile—small but genuine. "I could teach you. Basic maintenance isn't hard."

The casual offer dangles between us, loaded with implication. Teaching takes time. Time means staying.

"Maybe," I say noncommittally, though something in my chest tightens at the thought.

He finishes with the coolant, then wipes his hands on a rag. "Want to start her up?"

I slide off the stool, taking the keys he offers. Our fingers brush, and even without the heat-madness, electricity zips up my arm. His eyes darken momentarily, nostrils flaring as he catches my scent. My heat may be temporarily dormant, but the connection between us remains.

I climb into Betsy's driver's seat, suddenly reluctant to turn the key. If the car starts, I have no reason to stay. No excuse to remain in Sanctuary, in this garage, with this unexpectedly gentle alpha who treats me like I matter.

"Go ahead," Colt encourages, standing back.

I turn the key. The engine catches immediately, purring more smoothly than it has in years. No ominous knocking. No dashboard warning lights. Colt's fixed her completely.

"Sounds good," I say, trying to muster enthusiasm.

"Should get you where you need to go." He leans against the fender, studying me. "Wherever that is."

His unspoken words fill the space between us. Am I leaving?

Twenty-four hours ago, the answer would have been automatic. Of course I'm leaving. I always leave. It's what I do—what I've done for eight years. Never staying long enough to form attachments. Never risking rejection by trying to belong.

But now...

I turn off the engine, the sudden silence deafening. Through the windshield, I watch Colt close the hood, his movements efficient but unhurried. He doesn't press me for an answer or rush me to a decision. Just gives me space to think, to feel, to choose.

For the first time in years, I'm not immediately planning my escape route. For the first time ever, the thought of staying somewhere doesn't feel like a trap closing around me. It feels like... possibility.

The realization terrifies me. And yet, as I watch Colt move around the garage, as I breathe in the scent of oil and metal and alpha that's becoming strangely familiar, I find myself considering something I've never allowed before:

What if I stayed, just for a little while?

My heat will return soon enough. That's the practical excuse—I can't safely travel during heat. But beneath that convenient reasoning lies a deeper truth. Something about this grumpy alpha mechanic and his quiet garage feels more like home than anywhere I've been in eight years of running.

10

— · —

My car is fixed. The bill is paid—Colt waved off half the cost despite my protests. There's nothing keeping me in Sanctuary except the decision I can't seem to make. I sit in Betsy's driver's seat, key in the ignition, maps spread across the passenger side, but I haven't turned the key. Haven't plotted my next destination. Haven't done anything but stare through the windshield at Colt, who's giving me space by busying himself with another customer's vehicle, though his eyes flick to me every few minutes.

The familiar restlessness that usually propels me forward is strangely absent. In its place, a new feeling—something like longing, but heavier. More substantial.

My heat will return by nightfall. I can feel it simmering beneath the surface, a slow-building warmth in my core. Logic says I should either leave now, while I have clarity, or commit to staying through the full cycle. There's no safe in-between.

I fold the maps, tuck them into the glove compartment, and step out of the car.

Colt straightens immediately, wiping his hands on a rag. His expression is carefully neutral, but his scent gives him away—hope and anxiety mingling with his natural alpha musk.

"Decided?" he asks, voice deliberately casual.

I lean against Betsy's hood, arms crossed over my chest like a shield. "I'm tired, Colt."

His brow furrows. "Your heat—"

"Not that kind of tired." I look past him, out the open garage door to the main street of Sanctuary. People walk by—ordinary people living ordinary lives in one place. "I'm tired of drifting. Of never belonging anywhere. Of being the perpetual stranger."

He says nothing, just watches me with those intense amber eyes.

"Eight years," I continue, the words spilling out now. "Eight years of nowhere being home. Of keeping everyone at arm's length because what's the point of connections when you're just passing through?"

"Why stay on the move?" he asks quietly.

"Because…" I search for the truth, not the glib answers I usually give. "Because if I never try to belong, I can't be rejected. Can't be hurt when it inevitably falls apart."

Colt steps closer, entering my space but not touching me. "And now?"

"Now I'm standing at a crossroads." I meet his gaze directly. "And for the first time, the idea of staying somewhere doesn't feel like a trap."

"Here." Not a question. A statement.

I nod. "Something about this place feels... different."

"The place?" His voice drops lower. "Or the people?"

My chest tightens. "Maybe both."

Colt rubs the back of his neck, clearly struggling with words. He's not a man who expresses himself easily—I've learned that much about him already.

"I don't want you to go," he finally says, the admission gruff but sincere.

Four simple words that crack something open inside me.

"Because of the mate pull?" I ask, needing clarity. "Because your rut and my heat aligned?"

"That's part of it." He gestures vaguely between us. "This connection—it's rare. But it's not just biology."

"No," I agree softly. "It's not."

In the silence that follows, I study his face—the strong line of his jaw, the tiny wrinkles at the corners of his eyes, the scar above his eyebrow. A face I've known for less than forty-eight hours but already feels important, essential.

"If I stayed," I say carefully, "what would that even look like? I have no job, no place to live, barely enough money for gas."

"We'd figure it out." He sounds so certain, so steady. "Marge at the diner is always hiring. You could stay with—" He stops, hesitating.

"With you?" I finish.

"If you wanted. No pressure. There's rooms above the diner too."

I try to imagine it—waking up in his apartment, having coffee before he heads down to the garage, building a routine in this small town. It's both terrifying and strangely appealing.

"I've never really had a real job," I admit. "Just gigs, temporary things."

"Marge doesn't care about resumes. Just needs someone reliable who can carry plates and be nice to customers." He pauses. "You'd be good at the second part."

I snort. "You think I'm nice?"

"I think you're..." He searches for the word. "Sunny. Like your name."

The simple observation touches me more than flowery compliments ever could.

"What about this?" I gesture between us. "Whatever is happening here?"

"We take it slow," he says. "After your heat passes. See if what we feel is real beyond the biology."

"Slow," I repeat, testing the word. Not a concept I'm familiar with—I've always lived fast, moved fast, left fast. "I could try slow."

A ghost of a smile touches his lips. "The town grows on you. Folks mind their own business, mostly. Let you be who you are."

"And who am I, Colt?" The question slips out, more vulnerable than I intended.

"Still figuring that out, I think." He reaches out, tucking a strand of hair behind my ear, the touch gentle. "But I'd like to see who you become when you're not running."

His words hit with unexpected force. Who am I when I'm not defined by movement, by transience? I've never stayed still long enough to find out.

"What if it doesn't work?" I voice my deepest fear. "What if I stay and then everything falls apart?"

"Then you get back in your car and drive away." He shrugs, but his eyes are intense. "But at least you'll know you tried something different."

Something different. Something terrifying. Something potentially wonderful.

"My heat will be back tonight," I say, practical concerns intruding.

"I know." His pupils dilate slightly at the reminder. "We'll handle it however you want. Together or separate. Your choice."

Again with the choices. The respect. The lack of assumption or entitlement I've encountered with other alphas.

"Together," I say decisively. "That part worked pretty well."

His laugh is unexpected and delightful—a deep, rusty sound like he doesn't use it often. "Yeah, it did."

A customer enters the garage, breaking our bubble of intimacy. Colt nods professionally, stepping back from me. "Be right with you," he tells the older man, then turns back to me. "Think about it. No pressure. Whatever you decide, I'll respect it."

I watch him walk away, greeting the customer with a handshake. He moves with confidence here—a man who knows his place in the world, who belongs somewhere. I've never had that. Never even thought I wanted it.

But watching him now, I wonder if belonging isn't about place at all. Maybe it's about people. About finding someone who sees you—really sees you—and wants you to stay anyway.

I run my fingers along Betsy's hood, the metal warm from the sun. My faithful companion for years of running. But maybe, just maybe, it's time to see what happens when I stand still.

Not forever. I can't promise forever. But for now—for this moment—the road can wait.

I walk toward the garage office, decision made. At least for today, I'm staying in Sanctuary. With Colt. To see what happens when a drifter drops anchor, however temporarily, in the harbor of a gruff alpha mechanic who makes me feel safe for the first time in my adult life.

It might be the biggest adventure yet.

11

— • —

The first week at Marge's Diner passes in a blur of dropped plates, confused orders, and sore feet. Marge herself is a force of nature—sixty-something with flame-red hair that's definitely not natural and the mouth of a sailor who's seen some shit. She hires me on the spot after Colt walks me in, not bothering with references or experience. "You got a pulse and you're not afraid of work? You're hired." Just like that, I have a job. A real one, with a schedule and a name tag and everything. The concept is so foreign I keep waiting for someone to realize I don't belong and kick me out.

By week two, I've stopped breaking things and learned the regulars' orders by heart. There's Sheriff Hayes who likes his eggs over-easy and his bacon extra crispy. The trio of retired teachers who split a piece of pie three ways every afternoon. The high school kids who pile in after school, ordering nothing but fries and milkshakes, leaving their tables sticky with spilled soda and wadded napkins.

They all eye me curiously at first—the stranger, the outsider, the omega who smells faintly of their town's reclusive alpha mechanic. The questions come obliquely, casually tossed between bites of pancakes or sips of coffee.

"Passing through?" (Not anymore.)

"Staying with family?" (Don't have any.)

"Known Colt long?" (Define 'long'.)

I deflect with ease, turning questions back on the askers, learning their stories instead of sharing mine. It's a skill honed by years of being the perpetual newcomer—make them talk about themselves, and they forget to pry into your business.

But something strange happens in week three. The questions taper off. People start greeting me by name when they come in. Sheriff Hayes asks how I'm settling in like he actually cares about the answer. Marge stops watching me like I might bolt and starts teaching me how to make her famous pies.

"You've got good hands for pastry," she tells me, watching me crimp a perfect edge. "Gentle but confident."

I think of all the places those hands have been—clinging to the backs of pickup trucks, gripping steering wheels on midnight escapes, wrapped around pool cues in dive bars, and most recently, digging into Colt's shoulders as he moved above me. Gentle is not a word I'd have ever applied to myself.

Colt picks me up after each shift, though the garage is only two blocks away and I'm perfectly capable of walking. He pretends it's casual, just happening to finish work at the same time, but I know better. He's staking a claim, letting the town see us together. Making it clear that the new omega waitress isn't unprotected.

I should hate it. Should bristle at the possessiveness, the traditional alpha behavior. But there's something undeniably comforting about sliding into his truck at the end of a long day, about the quiet rumble of his voice asking how my shift went, about the way his hand sometimes finds mine across the seat.

We're taking it slow, as promised. After my heat passed—three days of intensity that left us both exhausted and oddly closer—we established boundaries. I'm staying in the apartment above the diner for now, though I spend most nights at Colt's place. We're learning each other outside the haze of pheromones and biological imperatives.

I learn that Colt reads voraciously, everything from technical manuals to history books. That he can't cook anything more complicated than eggs but makes truly excellent coffee. That he hums under his breath when he's working on engines, usually old country songs his uncle used to play.

He learns that I'm a night owl who struggles to function before 10 AM. That I can fold myself into impossibly small spaces—a skill developed sleeping in my car. That I know every word to every ABBA song ever recorded, a quirk inherited from the only decent foster mom I ever had.

Small details. Mundane revelations. The building blocks of something I've never allowed myself before.

The town watches our courtship with poorly disguised interest. I catch whispers, notice the speculative glances when we walk down Main Street together. Colt seems oblivious, but I know he's aware. He's just better at ignoring it.

"Does it bother you?" I ask one night as we eat takeout on his couch. "Everyone talking about us?"

He shrugs, chopsticks paused halfway to his mouth. "Small towns run on gossip. They'll find something new to talk about eventually."

"They're saying I tamed the grumpy mechanic."

That gets a snort. "You haven't tamed shit."

"No?" I poke his ribs with my foot. "You went to the school fundraiser last week. Marge nearly fainted when you bought a raffle ticket."

"I went because you were working the booth."

"Still. You're... integrating."

He considers this, head tilted. "Maybe I am."

The admission hangs between us—evidence of how we're changing each other in small but significant ways. I'm putting down tentative roots. He's emerging from his self-imposed isolation. Both terrifying. Both necessary.

Four weeks after my car broke down, I wake with the telltale warmth spreading through my lower abdomen. Not a cramp, not yet, but a harbinger—my heat approaching again, right on schedule. The realization brings less panic than before. I have a job now. A place to stay. An alpha who's proven himself trustworthy.

That evening, Colt senses it immediately when I enter the garage. His nostrils flare, pupils dilating slightly as he looks up from the engine he's working on.

"Two days," I say, answering his unspoken question. "Maybe three."

He nods, wiping his hands clean. "We should talk about it."

We sit in his kitchen, the scene of our first real conversation a month ago. So much has changed since then. I've changed.

"Last time," Colt says carefully, "it was biology. Heat and rut and mate pull. No real choice involved."

I nod, sensing where this is going.

"This time could be different." His eyes meet mine, steady and serious. "If you want it to be."

"Different how?"

"A conscious choice. Not just satisfying a biological need, but… choosing each other. Completely."

He means the claiming bite. The permanent bond. The thing that would tie us together in the most primal, irrevocable way.

"That's a big step," I say, my heart racing. "For someone who's spent her adult life avoiding attachment."

"I know." His hand finds mine across the table. "I'm not pushing. Just putting it out there. As an option."

I stare at our joined hands—his large and calloused, mine smaller but just as work-roughened now. A month ago, I was drifting, rootless, convinced that belonging anywhere was a fantasy not meant for me. Now I have a job where people know my name, regular customers who smile when I approach their tables, an alpha whose scent makes me feel safe rather than threatened.

I have, against all odds and expectations, found a home I never knew I was looking for.

"What if I mess it up?" I voice my deepest fear. "I don't exactly have a great track record with permanence."

"We'll mess up," Colt says with absolute certainty. "Both of us. That's how this works. We mess up, we fight, we figure it out."

"Simple as that?"

"Nothing simple about it." His thumb traces patterns on my palm. "But worth trying. If you want to."

I look at him—really look at him. The man who fixed my car and inadvertently stopped my running. Who respects my boundaries but challenges my fears. Whose alpha scent has become synonymous with safety in my mind.

"I want to," I say, the words both terrifying and liberating. "When my heat comes, I want the claiming bite. I want to complete the bond."

His smile—rare and beautiful—breaks across his face like sunrise. "Yeah?"

"Yeah." I squeeze his hand. "Let's see what happens when a drifter finally drops anchor."

Outside the window, Sanctuary's main street hums with evening activity. For the first time, it doesn't look like a temporary backdrop to me. It looks like a place I might belong.

12

The apartment above the garage feels different tonight—charged with intention rather than desperate need. Colt has cleaned the place, lit a few candles he'll later deny purchasing specifically for this occasion. The windows are cracked to let in the cool evening breeze, curtains dancing gently. My heat is present but controlled, a slow-building warmth rather than the inferno of last time. This isn't about biology hijacking our bodies. This is choice. This is us, Sunny and Colt, deciding to tie our lives together in the most ancient, primal way.

"Nervous?" Colt asks, standing by the bedroom door as I take in his preparations—fresh sheets, water bottles on the nightstand, even flowers in a chipped mug that makes me smile.

"A little," I admit, because we're past pretending with each other. "You?"

"Terrified." His honesty disarms me completely. "Never thought I'd do this."

"Make an honest omega out of someone?" I tease, hiding my own vulnerability behind humor.

"Find someone worth claiming." He steps closer, one hand cupping my cheek. "Worth being claimed by."

His amber eyes hold mine, searching for doubts, for hesitation. He won't find any. I made my decision days ago, in quiet moments between diner shifts and late-night conversations. This gruff, gentle alpha has become my safe harbor, and I'm ready to drop anchor.

"I want this," I say, turning to kiss his palm. "I want you."

The words break something open between us. Colt's lips find mine, the kiss deep but unhurried. We have time now—no desperate rush of heat-madness, no primal urgency. His hands slide under my shirt, mapping my skin with careful attention, learning me in ways our first frenzied coupling didn't allow.

I guide him toward the bed, our clothing shed piece by piece along the way. Each new expanse of skin revealed feels like a gift, a discovery. I trace the scar that runs along his ribs—a motorcycle accident when he was twenty. He kisses the small tattoo on my hip—a compass rose, inked after my first year on the road.

"Beautiful," he murmurs against my skin. "Every inch of you."

No one has ever looked at me the way Colt does—like I'm precious, like I matter, like I'm someone worth keeping. I pull him closer, needing his weight, his warmth, the solid reality of him against me.

We fall to the bed in a tangle of limbs, no longer strangers but not yet fully known to each other. There's still so much to learn, to explore. His hands find the places that make me gasp—the sensitive spot behind my ear, the curve of my waist, the inner crease of my thigh. I discover he melts when I run my nails lightly down his back, that he has a ticklish spot just below his ribs, that the juncture of his neck and shoulder makes him growl when I bite it gently.

"I want to take my time with you," he says, voice rough with desire. "Not like before."

"We have all night," I remind him, arching as his fingers trace patterns on my inner thighs. "All the nights."

The promise of his words lingers, electric and heavy, like a storm front waiting to break. I feel it in the way he looks at me—soft, reverent, a thousand unsaid things shimmering in the space between our bodies. He kneels at the edge of the bed while I sprawl above him, already flushed and slick and aching. The room is shadowed, candlelight flickering over plaster and old brick, the world outside hushed and irrelevant.

Colt lets his hands linger on my shins, fingers splayed, the calluses a rasping counterpoint to my skin. He doesn't rush. He kisses the hollow at my knee, the freckled skin above it, then moves upward, mouth dragging heat wherever it goes.

My hips squirm, restless, and he steadies me with a firm grip.

"Easy," he murmurs, voice rougher than sandpaper. "Let me."

I let him. I want his touch—have wanted it, even needed it, every hour since that first, wild night. But it's different now. The desperation's been replaced by something deeper, a need to memorize, to claim, to savor.

He spreads my thighs and lowers his head. The first brush of his tongue is soft, exploratory, just a taste. It sends lightning through my nerves; I gasp, arching for more. He doesn't oblige—not yet. Instead, he circles, licks, bites lightly at the inside of my thigh, making me writhe.

"Colt—" I start, but the rest is lost to sensation.

He grins up at me, wicked and knowing. "You said all night, Sunny. I'm holding you to it."

And then he finally—finally—gives me what I want. His mouth covers me, hot and relentless, tongue parting me with a kind of reverence. I thread my fingers into his hair, desperate for an anchor, and he lets me guide him. He hums, the vibrations making everything sharper. I'm close in seconds, the promise of release an electric wire beneath my skin.

Just as I crest, he pulls away, leaving me gasping, teetering on the edge. My thighs clamp around his head, trying to force him back, but he just laughs, low and guttural, and presses a kiss to my hip.

"You bastard," I whisper, half-laughing, half-sobbing.

He climbs up the bed, settling between my knees, arms braced on either side of my head. His mouth is slick, lips parted, pupils blown wide. "It's better like this," he says. "When you finally let go, you'll feel it everywhere."

I want to argue, to demand, but he kisses me hard, swallowing the protest. His hand—big, rough, gentle—slides down, fingers stroking where his tongue left off. He finds my rhythm, matches it, keeps me hovering just below oblivion.

I claw at his shoulders, leave crescent marks on his back, but he just grins, the smug bastard, and keeps me right where he wants me: trembling, desperate, held in place by the promise of more.

His other hand drifts up, thumb tracing my cheekbone. "You're beautiful like this," he says, and I almost believe it.

"Then let me come," I pant, nails digging in.

He dips his head, brushing his nose along my jaw, my neck, the shell of my ear. "Not yet."

"Tease," I accuse, breathless.

"Patient," he corrects, moving up my body to claim my mouth again. "Want to be inside you when you come. Want to feel it."

I wrap my legs around his waist, pulling him closer. "Then get inside me already."

He laughs—that rare, beautiful sound I'm slowly coaxing from him more often. "So demanding."

"You have no idea."

He enters me slowly, both of us groaning at the perfect friction. This position lets me see his face, watch the pleasure transform his features as he seats himself fully inside me. We fit together like we were designed for each other—maybe we were, my omega to his alpha, a biological lock and key that somehow transcends mere instinct.

"Okay?" he asks, always checking, always making sure.

"Perfect," I breathe, rolling my hips to take him deeper. "Move, Colt. Please."

He starts slow, impossibly slow, his hips rolling with deliberate care. Each stroke lands deep, a steady, thorough claiming that makes me keen and clutch at his back. The rhythm is not the frantic, heat-driven rut of that first night in the garage, all claws and bitten lips, but something else entirely—an intentional, measured dance, a kind of music with a time signature known only to the two of us. With every thrust, he's telling me something without words: that I'm safe, that I'm wanted, that I'm here, that I belong.

He watches my face as he moves inside me, his own features caught between hunger and awe, like he can't quite believe this is really happening. The candlelight halos him in gold, finds the streak of gray above his ear, makes him look ancient and brand new all at once. I feel every inch he gives me, every pulse and flex, and I answer back with my own—meeting him, urging him deeper, matching his slow, inexorable build.

When our bodies slip into a perfect lockstep, he brings my hand to his mouth and presses a reverent kiss to my knuckles before pinning it to the mattress. His fingers lace through mine, a silent promise stitched together with sweat and breath and the tension between our joined palms. For the first time in my life, the act of being held down doesn't feel like a trap. It feels like being anchored, like being claimed and cherished in the same moment.

The physical becomes a feedback loop—his hand, my pulse, the friction of our skin, the way his stubble scrapes my neck when he nuzzles close. The air grows thick with the scent of us: his musk, my sweat, the way our pheromones tangle and amplify, not overwhelming but exhilarating. As he thrusts, slow and relentless, the base of his cock drags against that spot inside me that sets off fireworks behind my eyelids. I gasp and arch and he catches my movement, pinning me open with a thigh and a growl, smiling into my open mouth.

"Still with me?" he asks, voice ragged.

I nod, breathless, the swell of pleasure rising and receding, building again like the sea. He's teasing me with the rhythm, edging me just short of climax before bringing me back down, like he wants to draw out every second, make it last. The anticipation is torture—delicious, sprawling torture—and I surrender to it, let him steer us both toward oblivion in slow, dizzying spirals.

He is inside me in every way that matters, and I am terrifyingly, beautifully alive.

I feel the shift in Colt just before he speaks. His hips falter, his hand tightens on mine, and his forehead drops to my shoulder.

"I never thought I'd find you," he murmurs against my ear, his rhythm faltering as we both near the edge. "Never thought I'd want this."

"Me neither," I gasp, feeling my release building. "Never wanted to belong anywhere. To anyone."

"And now?"

"Now I'm yours." The admission breaks free as my climax crashes over me, waves of pleasure radiating outward as my inner walls clench around him.

He follows me over, his release triggering the swelling of his knot, locking us together in the most primal way. As the pleasure crests, he buries his face in the curve of my neck, seeking the spot where my scent is strongest.

"May I?" he asks, teeth grazing the sensitive skin.

"Yes," I breathe, tilting my head to give him better access. "Make me yours."

His teeth break the skin as his knot locks fully, the twin sensations of pain and pleasure so intense that a second orgasm ripples through me. The claiming bite—the permanent mark that will announce to the world that I am mated, chosen, bonded. The mark I never thought I'd want or accept.

The mark that now feels like coming home.

Colt licks the wound gently, soothing the sting. His arms tighten around me, cradling me close as our breathing gradually slows. We're locked together by his knot, by the claiming bite, by something deeper and more complex than either—by choice.

"Did I hurt you?" he asks, voice rough with concern.

I shake my head, too overwhelmed for words. My fingers trace the spot where I'll leave my answering bite when his knot subsides—the reciprocal mark that will complete our bond.

"I never understood," I say finally, voice barely above a whisper. "Why people would choose this. Choose to be tied to one person, one place."

"And now?" His hand strokes my hair, gentle in a way his gruff exterior wouldn't suggest.

"Now I get it." I press a kiss to his chest, right over his heart. "It's not a cage. It's an anchor."

He considers this, his heartbeat steady beneath my ear. "You won't get restless? Miss the road?"

"Oh, I will." I laugh softly. "I'm not suddenly a different person. I'll still want adventures, still crave movement sometimes."

"We can do that," he says immediately. "Take trips. Explore. I'm not trying to clip your wings, Sunny."

The simple acceptance of who I am—wanderlust and all—fills me with a warmth that has nothing to do with heat. "And you won't mind sharing your space? Having someone disrupt your solitude?"

His arms tighten around me. "Already adjusted to that. Kind of like it, actually."

"Even when I sing ABBA songs in the shower and leave my clothes everywhere?"

"Even then." He presses a kiss to my forehead. "Though the ABBA thing might be a dealbreaker."

I pinch his side, making him yelp. "Too late. You're stuck with me now."

"Guess I am." The satisfaction in his voice makes me smile against his skin.

We fall silent, content to simply exist together as his knot gradually subsides. Outside, Sanctuary settles into evening rhythms—distant music from the bar down the street, the occasional car passing, the hum of small-town life continuing around us. For the first time, I don't feel like an observer watching from the outside. I feel like a participant, a resident, a part of something.

"What happens now?" I ask, not really expecting an answer.

"Now we figure it out," Colt says simply. "Day by day. Together."

Together. The word no longer frightens me as it once did. In Colt's arms, with his claiming bite fresh on my neck and his scent surrounding me, "together" feels like freedom rather than confinement. Like possibility rather than limitation.

As sleep claims us, tangled in each other's arms, I have one last coherent thought. Sometimes, the greatest adventure isn't found on the open road, but in the act of staying still long enough to be found.

Find out what happens next in Sanctuary with Ethan and Avery's story in The Alpha Firefighter! (Continue to the next page for a Bonus Epilogue.)

Want more of Colt and Sunny? Sign up for the Ash Jade newsletter and download a free bonus scene today! Click here: The Alpha Mechanic Bonus Scene.

(https://ashjadeauthor.com/alphamechanicbonus)

— · —

Bonus Epilogue

Ethan

The station is quiet tonight—too quiet for my liking. I pace between the trucks, trailing my fingers along cold metal, waiting for something to happen. Five hours into a twelve-hour shift and the most exciting call was Mrs. Henderson's cat stuck in her chimney again. But there's something in the air tonight, a pressure building like the moments before lightning strikes. My skin prickles with it, and I can't shake the feeling that everything's about to change.

"Rawlins, you're wearing a path in the floor." Captain Rivera doesn't look up from his crossword puzzle, but his nostrils flare slightly. He can smell my restlessness. "Go clean something if you need to move."

"Already cleaned the equipment twice." I roll my shoulders, trying to dislodge the itch crawling beneath my skin. "Just feeling—"

"Antsy. I can tell." Now he does look up, dark eyes narrowing. "Your rut's not for another two weeks."

I bristle at the mention. "It's not that."

"Then sit your ass down before I assign you bathroom duty."

The captain's alpha command doesn't carry any real force behind it—not with me—but I drop into a chair anyway, out of respect more than submission. That's how things work in Sanctuary. Even between alphas, there's a code. Respect the chain, but no one breaks another's will.

I drum my fingers against the table, glancing at the dispatch panel's silent lights. From the kitchen, the clatter of dishes and low chatter drifts in—Garcia and Tanner arguing about the best way to grill a steak. Everyday normal. So why does my pulse feel like it's counting down to something?

"You good?" Mason drops into the chair beside me, sliding a mug of coffee across the table. He's the only other alpha on our shift, though newer to the force. Still learning Sanctuary's unwritten rules.

"Fine." I wrap my hands around the mug, grateful for something to hold onto. "Just one of those nights."

Mason's nostrils flare slightly, scenting the air between us. "Bullshit. You smell like a thunderstorm."

I growl low in my throat—a warning he ignores with a grin.

"Hey, no judgment. We all get those weird alpha moments. Like my cousin Barry who swore he could sense earthquakes before they hit." Mason leans back in his chair. "Turned out he just had gas."

Despite myself, I snort. Mason has that effect—cutting through tension with his particular brand of stupid. It's why we work well together, why the captain paired us up despite the conventional wisdom about two alphas on the same crew.

"It's not gas." I take a sip of coffee, grimacing at the burnt taste. Mason can't make coffee worth shit. "Just feels like we're due for something. Been too quiet lately."

"Don't jinx it, asshole." He kicks my chair. "Some of us appreciate quiet shifts where nothing burns down and nobody dies."

The scanner on the wall hisses with static, and we both freeze. For a second, there's just white noise—then dispatch's voice crackles through, cool and professional.

"Station 42, we have reports of smoke at the old Milligan warehouse on County Line. Caller says they saw flames on the east side."

I'm on my feet before the message finishes, something electric shooting through my veins. The Milligan warehouse has been abandoned for years—a hulking concrete shell at the edge of town, just inside Sanctuary's borders.

"That's weird," Mason says, already moving toward the lockers. "Nobody's been out there in—"

"Squatters maybe," Captain Rivera cuts in, grabbing his radio. "Or those kids again. Either way, gear up."

The station erupts into controlled chaos as everyone moves to their positions. I'm at my locker in three strides, pulling out my turnout gear with practiced efficiency. But as I reach for my helmet, a scent hits me—faint and impossible, like a memory of something I've never actually smelled before.

Wild honey. Cedar. Blood.

I freeze, one arm in my jacket.

"Rawlins! Move your ass!" The captain's voice snaps me back.

I finish gearing up on autopilot, my brain scrambling to make sense of what just happened. There's no way I could smell anything from the warehouse at this distance. No way my alpha senses are that sharp. And yet, the phantom scent lingers in my nose, making my gums ache where my canines want to drop.

Three minutes later, I'm in the truck, compressed between Mason and Tanner as we tear out of the station, sirens wailing. The captain's driving, and Garcia's riding shotgun, already coordinating with dispatch for additional details.

"Update says we've got confirmed flames now," Garcia calls back. "No word on occupancy."

My knee bounces with nervous energy. That damn scent won't leave me, growing stronger with every mile closer we get to the warehouse. It's making my alpha instincts go haywire—protect, claim, defend all tangling together in a mess I can't sort out.

"You look like you're about to jump out of your skin," Mason mutters, low enough that only I can hear.

"I'm fine."

"Yeah, right." He eyes me carefully. "Seriously, what's going on? You've never been squirrelly on a call before."

I clench my jaw, unwilling to voice the madness churning inside me. How do I explain that I think I'm smelling someone who isn't there yet? Someone whose scent is calling to something primal in me?

"Just focused," I manage.

Mason doesn't buy it, but he drops it as we round the final bend in the road and the warehouse comes into view. Flames are visible now, licking up one corner of the building, orange against the night sky. Not a massive blaze yet, but growing fast.

"Shit," the captain mutters. "Dispatch, we're going to need backup. This is bigger than reported."

As we pull into the gravel lot, my vision tunnels. The phantom scent hits me full force now—no longer a hint but a punch to the gut. Honey. Cedar. Fear. Pain. Omega.

I'm out of the truck before it fully stops, my body moving on its own.

"Rawlins!" The captain's alpha command slices through the air. "Procedure! Don't you dare—"

But I'm already assessing the building, noting entry points, mapping the flames in my head. Someone's in there. Someone important. The knowledge sits in my chest with absolute certainty.

"There's an omega inside," I cut him off, voice rough. "East side, second floor."

The captain stares at me. "How the hell could you possibly know that?"

"I can smell them." The words sound insane even to my own ears, but I know I'm right. "Captain, I know what I'm sensing."

Rivera studies my face, twenty years of firefighting experience warring with the instincts of a pack alpha who knows when another alpha is dead certain about something.

"Garcia, Tanner—take the west entrance, control the perimeter. Mason, with me on the water line." He points at me. "You—two minutes to do a sweep of the east side. In and out. You find anyone, you call it in immediately. You don't play hero."

I nod, already moving, pulling my mask into place. The roar of the fire grows louder as I approach, but it's nothing compared to the roar in my blood. The omega's scent is clearer with each step, wrapped in fear and smoke.

At the side entrance, I pause, checking the door for heat. It's warm but manageable. I push through, stepping into the hazy interior of the warehouse. The smoke isn't too thick on this level yet, but it's only a matter of time.

"Fire department! Call out if you can hear me!" My voice echoes in the cavernous space.

Nothing but the crackle of flames.

I move deeper, scanning methodically despite the pull in my chest urging me upstairs. The first floor appears empty—just concrete floors and graffitied walls. At the metal staircase, I pause, radioing in.

"Rawlins to command. First floor clear, moving to second level."

"Copy that. One minute, Rawlins. Then you're out."

I take the stairs two at a time, the metal hot even through my gloves. At the top, the smoke is thicker, rolling along the ceiling. I crouch lower, scanning the open space. Most of the second floor is one large room, with a few partitioned offices along one wall.

That's when I hear it—a soft whimper, nearly lost under the fire's growl.

I move toward the sound, toward the back office with its door half-closed. The scent is overwhelming now—omega in distress, calling to every protective instinct I possess.

"Fire department! I'm here to help!" I push the door open.

In the corner, curled against the wall, is a woman. She's conscious but barely, her face streaked with soot, dark hair plastered to her forehead. When she looks up, her eyes widen with equal parts hope and terror.

The moment our eyes meet, everything inside me shifts, locks into place. The world narrows to this single point in space, to her. My omega. Mine to protect. Mine to save.

I don't even know her name, but I know with bone-deep certainty that nothing in my life will ever be the same.

Find out what happens next with Ethan and Avery in The Alpha Firefighter!

ALSO BY ASH JADE

Read more from Ash Jade
Short, binge-worthy omegaverse romances where instinct burns hot and love always wins.

Salt and Timber Coast Universe

Welcome to the Salt & Timber Coast.
A rain-bound peninsula where protection is steady, bonds are chosen, and love means staying.

Blackwater Bears

A quiet inland pack where bear shifters offer shelter, endurance, and a home that holds.

The Starfall Ridge Quick Reads Series

Welcome to Starfall Ridge.
*Where the crater sparks scents, fate strikes fast,
and no one escapes the pull of a mate.*

The Yule Curse Series

*Four fated nights. Four cursed alphas. One winter
where heat burns brighter than fire.*

The Touch Her and Die Series

*In a world ruled by dominance, instinct, and the
pull of fate, every story begins with danger—and
ends with devotion.*

The Sanctuary Pack Series

Welcome to Sanctuary.
*A hidden mountain town where omegas come to
heal—and alphas learn what it means to protect.*

About Ash Jade

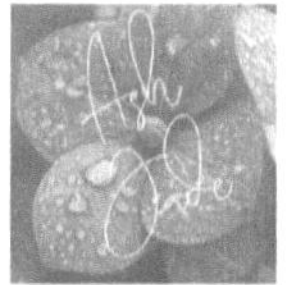

Ash Jade writes trope-packed omegaverse romances full of heat, ruts, and fated mates — but always with heart. Her stories are fast, messy, and addictive, blending primal passion with emotional cores that make the bonds hit even harder. If you love bingeable romances where instinct tangles with feelings (and always ends in happily-ever-after), you've found your pack.

ashjadeauthor.com

www.ingramcontent.com/pod-product-compliance
Lightning Source LLC
Chambersburg PA
CBHW020048310726
48970CB00007B/2466